THE IGNOBLE
SAVAGES

THE IGNOBLE SAVAGES

by Evelyn E. Smith

Snaddra had but one choice in its fight to afford to live belowground—
underhandedly pretend theirs was an aboveboard society!

"Go Away from me, Skkiru," Larhgan said, pushing his hand off her arm. "A beggar does not associate with the high priestess of Snaddra."

"But the Earthmen aren't due for another fifteen minutes," Skkiru protested.

"Of what importance are fifteen minutes compared to eternity!" she exclaimed. Her lovely eyes fuzzed softly with emotion. "You don't seem to realize, Skkiru, that this isn't just a matter of minutes or hours. It's forever."

"Forever!" He looked at her incredulously. "You mean we're going to keep this up as a permanent thing? You're joking!"

Bbulas groaned, but Skkiru didn't care about that. The sad, sweet way Larhgan shook her beautiful head disturbed him much more, and when she said, "No, Skkiru, I am not joking," a tiny pang of doubt and apprehension began to quiver in his second smallest left toe.

"This is, in effect, good-by," she continued. "We shall see each other again, of course, but only from a distance. On feast days, perhaps you may be permitted to kiss the hem of my robe . . . but that will be all."

Skkiru turned to the third person present in the council chamber. "Bbulas, this is your fault! It was all your idea!"

There was regret on the Dilettante's thin face—an obviously insincere regret, the younger man knew, since he was well aware how Bbulas had always felt about the girl.

5

THE IGNOBLE SAVAGES

"I am sorry, Skkiru," Bbulas intoned. "I had fancied you understood. This is not a game we are playing, but a new way of life we are adopting. A necessary way of life, if we of Snaddra are to keep on living at all."

"It's not that I don't love you, Skkiru," Larhgan put in gently, "but the welfare of our planet comes first."

*

She had been seeing too many of the Terrestrial fictapes from the library, Skkiru thought resentfully. There was too damn much Terran influence on this planet. And this new project was the last straw.

No longer able to control his rage and grief, he turned a triple somersault in the air with rage. "Then why was I made a beggar and she the high priestess? You arranged that purposely, Bbulas. You—"

"Now, Skkiru," Bbulas said wearily, for they had been through all this before, "you know that all the ranks and positions were distributed by impartial lot, except for mine, and, of course, such jobs as could carry over from the civilized into the primitive."

Bbulas breathed on the spectacles he was wearing, as contact lenses were not considered backward enough for the kind of planet Snaddra was now supposed to be, and attempted to wipe them dry on his robe. However, the thick, jewel-studded embroidery got in his way and so he was forced to lift the robe and wipe all three of the lenses on the smooth, soft, spun metal of his top underskirt.

"After all," he went on speaking as he wiped, "I have to be high priest, since I organized this culture and am the only one here qualified to administer it. And, as the president himself concurred in these arrangements, I hardly think you—a mere private citizen—have the right to question them."

"Just because you went to school in another solar system," Skkiru said, whirling with anger, "you think you're so smart!"

6

"I won't deny that I do have educational and cultural advantages which were, unfortunately, not available to the general populace of this planet. However, even under the old system, I was always glad to utilize my superior attainments as Official Dilettante for the good of all and now—"

"Sure, glad to have a chance to rig this whole setup so you could break up things between Larhgan and me. You've had your eye on her for some time."

Skkiru coiled his antennae at Bbulas, hoping the insult would provoke him into an unbecoming whirl, but the Dilettante remained calm. One of the chief outward signs of Terran-type training was self-control and Bbulas had been thoroughly terranized.

I hate Terrestrials, Skkiru said to himself. *I hate Terra.* The quiver of anxiety had risen up his leg and was coiling and uncoiling in his stomach. He hoped it wouldn't reach his antennae—if he were to break down and psonk in front of Larhgan, it would be the final humiliation.

"Skkiru!" the girl exclaimed, rotating gently, for she, like her fiance—her erstwhile fiance, that was, for the new regime had caused all such ties to be severed—and every other literate person on the planet, had received her education at the local university. Although sound, the school was admittedly provincial in outlook and very poor in the emotional department. "One would almost think that the lots had some sort of divine intelligence behind them, because you certainly are behaving in a beggarly manner!"

"And I have already explained to you, Skkiru," Bbulas said, with a patience much more infuriating than the girl's anger, "that I had no idea of who was to become my high priestess. The lots chose Larhgan. It is, as the Earthmen say, kismet."

*

THE IGNOBLE SAVAGES

He adjusted the fall of his glittering robe before the great polished four-dimensional reflector that formed one wall of the chamber.

Kismet, Skkiru muttered to himself, *and a little sleight of hand.* But he didn't dare offer this conclusion aloud; the libel laws of Snaddra were very severe. So he had to fall back on a weak, "And I suppose it is kismet that makes us all have to go live out on the ground during the day, like—like savages."

"It is necessary," Bbulas replied without turning.

"Pooh," Skkiru said. "Pooh, *pooh*, POOH!"

Larhgan's dainty earflaps closed. "Skkiru! Such language!"

"As you said," Bbulas murmured, contemptuously coiling one antenna at Skkiru, "the lots chose well and if you touch me, Skkiru, we shall have another drawing for beggar and you will be made a metal-worker."

"But I can't work metal!"

"Then that will make it much worse for you than for the other outcasts," Bbulas said smugly, "because you will be a pariah without a trade."

"Speaking of pariahs, that reminds me, Skkiru, before I forget, I'd better give you back your grimpatch—" Larhgan handed the glittering bauble to him—"and you give me mine. Since we can't be betrothed any longer, you might want to give yours to some nice beggar girl."

"I don't want to give my grimpatch to some nice beggar girl!" Skkiru yelled, twirling madly in the air.

"As for me," she sighed, standing soulfully on her head, "I do not think I shall ever marry. I shall make the religious life my career. Are there going to be any saints in your mythos, Bbulas?"

"Even if there will be," Bbulas said, "you certainly won't qualify if you keep putting yourself into a position which not only represents a trait wholly out of keeping with the new culture, but is most unseemly with the high priestess's robes."

Larhgan ignored his unfeeling observations. "I shall set myself apart from mundane affairs," she vowed, "and I shall pretend to be happy, even though my heart will be breaking."

It was only at that moment that Skkiru realized just how outrageous the whole thing really was. There must be another solution to the planet's problem. "Listen—" he began, but just then excited noises filtered down from overhead. It was too late.

"Earth ship in view!" a squeaky voice called through the intercom. "Everybody topside and don't forget your shoes."

Except the beggar. Beggars went barefoot. Beggars suffered. Bbulas had made him beggar purposely, and the lots were a lot of slibwash.

"Hurry up, Skkiru."

*

Bbulas slid the ornate headdress over his antennae, which, already gilded and jeweled, at once seemed to become a part of it. He looked pretty damn silly, Skkiru thought, at the same time conscious of his own appearance—which was, although picturesque enough to delight romantic Terrestrial hearts, sufficiently wretched to charm the most hardened sadist.

"Hurry up, Skkiru," Bbulas said. "They mustn't suspect the existence of the city underground or we're finished before we've started."

"For my part, I wish we'd never started," Skkiru grumbled. "What was wrong with our old culture, anyway?"

That was intended as a rhetorical question, but Bbulas answered it anyway. He always answered questions; it had never seemed to penetrate his mind that school-days were long since over.

THE IGNOBLE SAVAGES

"I've told you a thousand times that our old culture was too much like the Terrans' own to be of interest to them," he said, with affected weariness. "After all, most civilized societies are basically similar; it is only primitive societies that differ sharply, one from the other—and we have to be different to attract Earthmen. They're pretty choosy. You've got to give them what they want, and that's what they want. Now take up your post on the edge of the field, try to look hungry, and remember this isn't for you or for me, but for Snaddra."

"For Snaddra," Larhgan said, placing her hand over her anterior heart in a gesture which, though devout on Earth—or so the fictapes seemed to indicate—was obscene on Snaddra, owing to the fact that certain essential organs were located in different areas in the Snaddrath than in the corresponding Terrestrial life-form. Already the Terrestrial influence was corrupting her, Skkiru thought mournfully. She had been such a nice girl, too.

"We may never meet on equal terms again, Skkiru," she told him, with a long, soulful glance that made his hearts sink down to his quivering toes, "but I promise you there will never be anyone else for me—and I hope that knowledge will inspire you to complete cooperation with Bbulas."

"If that doesn't," Bbulas said, "I have other methods of inspiration."

"All right," Skkiru answered sulkily. "I'll go to the edge of the field, and I'll speak broken Inter-galactic, and I'll forsake my normal habits and customs, and I'll even *beg*. But I don't have to like doing it, and I don't intend to like doing it."

All three of Larhgan's eyes fuzzed with emotion. "I'm proud of you, Skkiru," she said brokenly.

Bbulas sniffed. The three of them floated up to ground level in a triple silence.

10

EVELYN E. SMITH

*

"Alms, for the love of Ipsnadd," Skkiru chanted, as the two Terrans descended from the ship and plowed their way through the mud to meet a procession of young Snaddrath dressed in elaborate ceremonial costumes, and singing a popular ballad—to which less ribald, as well as less inspiring, words than the originals had been fitted by Bbulas, just in case, by some extremely remote chance, the Terrans had acquired a smattering of Snadd somewhere. Since neither party was accustomed to navigating mud, their progress was almost imperceptible.

"Alms, for the love of Ipsnadd," chanted Skkiru the beggar. His teeth chattered as he spoke, for the rags he wore had been custom-weatherbeaten for him by the planet's best tailor—now a pariah, of course, because Snadd tailors were, naturally, metal-workers—and the wind and the rain were joyously making their way through the demolished wires. Never before had Skkiru been on the surface of the planet, except to pass over, and he had actually touched it only when taking off and landing. The Snaddrath had no means of land transport, having previously found it unnecessary—but now both air-cars and self-levitation were on the prohibited list as being insufficiently primitive.

The outside was no place for a civilized human being, particularly in the wet season or—more properly speaking on Snaddra—the wetter season. Skkiru's feet were soaked with mud; not that the light sandals worn by the members of the procession appeared to be doing them much good, either. It gave him a kind of melancholy pleasure to see that the privileged ones were likewise trying to repress shivers. Though their costumes were rich, they were also scanty, particularly in the case of the females, for Earthmen had been reported by tape and tale to be humanoid.

11

THE IGNOBLE SAVAGES

As the mud clutched his toes, Skkiru remembered an idea he had once gotten from an old sporting fictape of Terrestrial origin and had always planned to experiment with, but had never gotten around to—the weather had always been so weathery, there were so many other more comfortable sports, Larhgan had wanted him to spend more of his leisure hours with her, and so on. However, he still had the equipment, which he'd salvaged from a wrecked air-car, in his apartment—and it was the matter of a moment to run down, while Bbulas was looking the other way, and get it.

Bbulas couldn't really object, Skkiru stilled the nagging quiver in his toe, because what could be more primitive than any form of land transport? And even though it took time to get the things, they worked so well that, in spite of the procession's head start, he was at the Earth ship long before the official greeters had reached it.

*

The newcomers were indeed humanoid, he saw. Only the peculiarly pasty color of their skins and their embarrassing lack of antennae distinguished them visibly from the Snaddrath. They were dressed much as the Snaddrath had been before they had adopted primitive garb.

In fact, the Terrestrials were quite decent-looking life-forms, entirely different from the foppish monsters Skkiru had somehow expected to represent the cultural ruling race. Of course, he had frequently seen pictures of them, but everyone knew how easily those could be retouched. Why, it was the Terrestrials themselves, he had always understood, who had invented the art of retouching—thus proving beyond a doubt that they had something to hide.

"Look, Raoul," the older of the two Earthmen said in Terran—which the Snaddrath were not, according to the master plan, supposed to understand, but which most of them did, for it was the

12

fashionable third language on most of the outer planets. "A beggar. Haven't seen one since some other chaps and I were doing a spot of field work on that little planet in the Arcturus system—what was its name? Glotch, that's it. Very short study, it turned out to be. Couldn't get more than a pamphlet out of it, as we were unable to stay long enough to amass enough material for a really definitive work. The natives tried to eat us, so we had to leave in somewhat of a hurry."

"Oh, they were cannibals?" the other Earthman asked, so respectfully that it was easy to deduce he was the subordinate of the two. "How horrible!"

"No, not at all," the other assured him. "They weren't human—another species entirely—so you could hardly call it cannibalism. In fact, it was quite all right from the ethical standpoint, but abstract moral considerations seemed less important to us than self-preservation just then. Decided that, in this case, it would be best to let the missionaries get first crack at them. Soften them up, you know."

"And the missionaries—did they soften them up, Cyril?"

"They softened up the missionaries, I believe." Cyril laughed. "Ah, well, it's all in the day's work."

"I hope these creatures are not man-eaters," Raoul commented, with a polite smile at Cyril and an apprehensive glance at the oncoming procession—*creatures indeed!* Skkiru thought, with a mental sniff. "We have come such a long and expensive way to study them that it would be indeed a pity if we also were forced to depart in haste. Especially since this is my first field trip and I would like to make good at it."

"Oh, you will, my boy, you will." Cyril clapped the younger man on the shoulder. "I have every confidence in your ability."

THE IGNOBLE SAVAGES

Either he was stupid, Skkiru thought, or he was lying, in spite of Bbulas' asseverations that untruth was unknown to Terrestrials—which had always seemed highly improbable, anyway. How could any intelligent life-form possibly stick to the truth all the time? It wasn't human; it wasn't even humanoid; it wasn't even polite.

"The natives certainly appear to be human enough," Raoul added, with an appreciative glance at the females, who had been selected for the processional honor with a view to reported Terrestrial tastes. "Some slight differences, of course—but, if two eyes are beautiful, three eyes can be fifty per cent lovelier, and chartreuse has always been my favorite color."

If they stand out here in the cold much longer, they are going to turn bright yellow. His own skin, Skkiru knew, had faded from its normal healthy emerald to a sickly celadon.

*

Cyril frowned and his companion's smile vanished, as if the contortion of his superior's face had activated a circuit somewhere. *Maybe the little one's a robot!* However, it couldn't be—a robot would be better constructed and less interested in females than Raoul.

"Remember," Cyril said sternly, "we must not establish undue rapport with the native females. It tends to detract from true objectivity."

"Yes, Cyril," Raoul said meekly.

Cyril assumed a more cheerful aspect "I should like to give this chap something for old times' sake. What do you suppose is the medium of exchange here?"

Money, Skkiru said to himself, but he didn't dare contribute this piece of information, helpful though it would be.

"How should I know?" Raoul shrugged.

"Empathize. Get in there, old chap, and start batting."

"Why not give him a bar of chocolate, then?" Raoul suggested grumpily. "The language of the stomach, like the language of love, is said to be a universal one."

"Splendid idea! I always knew you had it in you, Raoul!"

Skkiru accepted the candy with suitable—and entirely genuine—murmurs of gratitude. Chocolate was found only in the most expensive of the planet's delicacy shops—and now neither delicacy shops nor chocolate were to be found, so, if Bbulas thought he was going to save the gift to contribute it later to the Treasury, the "high priest" was off his rocker.

To make sure there would be no subsequent dispute about possession, Skkiru ate the candy then and there. Chocolate increased the body's resistance to weather, and never before had he had to endure so much weather all at once.

On Earth, he had heard, where people lived exposed to weather, they often sickened of it and passed on—which helped to solve the problem of birth control on so vulgarly fecund a planet. Snaddra, alas, needed no such measures, for its population—like its natural resources—was dwindling rapidly. Still, Skkiru thought, as he moodily munched on the chocolate, it would have been better to flicker out on their own than to descend to a subterfuge like this for nothing more than survival.

*

Being a beggar, Skkiru discovered, did give him certain small, momentary advantages over those who had been alloted higher ranks. For one thing, it was quite in character for him to tread curiously upon the strangers' heels all the way to the temple—a ramshackle affair, but then it had been run up in only three days—where the official reception was to be held. The principal difficulty was that, because of his equipment, he had a little trouble keeping himself from overshooting the strangers. And though Bbulas might frown menacingly at him—and not only for his forwardness—that was in character on both sides, too.

Nonetheless, Skkiru could not reconcile himself to his beggarhood, no matter how much he tried to comfort himself by thinking at least he wasn't a pariah like the unfortunate metal-workers who had to stand segregated from the rest by a chain of their own devising—a poetic thought, that was, but well in keeping with his beggarhood. Beggars were often poets, he believed, and poets almost always beggars. Since metal-working was the chief industry of Snaddra, this had provided the planet automatically with a large lowest caste. Bbulas had taken the easy way out.

Skkiru swallowed the last of the chocolate and regarded the "high priest" with a simple-minded mendicant's grin. However, there were volcanic passions within him that surged up from his toes when, as the wind and rain whipped through his scanty coverings, he remembered the snug underskirts Bbulas was wearing beneath his warm gown. They were metal, but they were solid. All the garments visible or potentially visible were of woven metal, because, although there was cloth on the planet, it was not politic for the Earthmen to discover how heavily the Snaddrath depended upon imports.

As the Earthmen reached the temple, Larhgan now appeared to join Bbulas at the head of the long flight of stairs that led to it. Although Skkiru had seen her in her priestly apparel before, it had not made the emotional impression upon him then that it did now, when, standing there, clad in beauty, dignity and warm clothes, she bade the newcomers welcome in several thousand words not too well chosen for her by Bbulas—who fancied himself a speech-writer as well as a speech-maker, for there was no end to the man's conceit.

The difference between her magnificent garments and his own miserable rags had their full impact upon Skkiru at this moment. He saw the gulf that had been dug between them and, for the first time in his short life, he felt the tormenting pangs of caste distinction. She looked so lovely and so remote.

" . . . and so you are most welcome to Snaddra, men of Earth," she was saying in her melodious voice. "Our resources may be small but our hearts are large, and what little we have, we offer with humility and with love. We hope that you will enjoy as long and as happy a stay here as you did on Nemeth. . . . "

Cyril looked at Raoul, who, however, seemed too absorbed in contemplating Larhgan's apparently universal charms to pay much attention to the expression on his companion's face.

" . . . and that you will carry our affection back to all the peoples of the Galaxy."

*

She had finished. And now Cyril cleared his throat. "Dear friends, we were honored by your gracious invitation to visit this fair planet, and we are honored now by the cordial reception you have given to us."

The crowd yoomped politely. After a slight start, Cyril went on, apparently deciding that applause was all that had been intended.

"We feel quite sure that we are going to derive both pleasure and profit from our stay here, and we promise to make our intensive analysis of your culture as painless as possible. We wish only to study your society, not to tamper with it in any way."

Ha, ha, Skkiru said to himself. *Ha, ha, ha!*

THE IGNOBLE SAVAGES

"But why is it," Raoul whispered in Terran as he glanced around out of the corners of his eyes, "that only the beggar wears mudshoes?"

"Shhh," Cyril hissed back. "We'll find out later, when we've established rapport. Don't be so impatient!"

Bbulas gave a sickly smile. Skkiru could almost find it in his hearts to feel sorry for the man.

"We have prepared our best hut for you, noble sirs," Bbulas said with great self-control, "and, by happy chance, this very evening a small but unusually interesting ceremony will be held outside the temple. We hope you will be able to attend. It is to be a rain dance."

"Rain dance!" Raoul pulled his macintosh together more tightly at the throat. "But why do you want rain? My faith, not only does it rain now, but the planet seems to be a veritable sea of mud. Not, of course," he added hurriedly as Cyril's reproachful eye caught his, "that it is not attractive mud. Finest mud I have ever seen. Such texture, such color, such aroma!"

Cyril nodded three times and gave an appreciative sniff.

"But," Raoul went on, "one can have too much of even such a good thing as mud. . . . "

The smile did not leave Bbulas' smooth face. "Yes, of course, honorable Terrestrials. That is why we are holding this ceremony. It is not a dance to bring on rain. It is a dance to *stop* rain."

He was pretty quick on the uptake, Skkiru had to concede. However, that was not enough. The man had no genuine organizational ability. In the time he'd had in which to plan and carry out a scheme for the improvement of Snaddra, surely he could have done better than this high-school theocracy. For one thing, he could have apportioned the various roles so that each person would be making a definite contribution to the society, instead of creating some positions plums, like the priesthood, and others prunes, like the beggarship.

What kind of life was that for an active, ambitious young man, standing around begging? And, moreover, from whom was Skkiru going to beg? Only the Earthmen, for the Snaddrath, no matter how much they threw themselves into the spirit of their roles, could not be so carried away that they would give handouts to a young man whom they had been accustomed to see basking in the bosom of luxury.

*

Unfortunately, the fees that he'd received in the past had not enabled him both to live well and to save, and now that his fortunes had been so drastically reduced, he seemed in a fair way of starving to death. It gave him a gentle, moody pleasure to envisage his own funeral, although, at the same time, he realized that Bbulas would probably have to arrange some sort of pension for him; he could not expect Skkiru's patriotism to extend to abnormal limits. A man might be willing to die for his planet in many ways—but wantonly starving to death as the result of a primitive affectation was hardly one of them.

All the same, Skkiru reflected as he watched the visitors being led off to the native hut prepared for them, how ignominious it would be for one of the brightest young architects on the planet to have to subsist miserably on the dole just because the world had gone aboveground. The capital had risen to the surface and the other cities would soon follow suit. Meanwhile, a careful system of tabus had been designed to keep the Earthmen from discovering the existence of those other cities.

He could, of course, emigrate to another part of the planet, to one of them, and stave off his doom for a while—but that would not be playing the game. Besides, in such a case, he wouldn't be able to see Larhgan.

As if all this weren't bad enough, he had been done an injury which struck directly at his professional pride. He hadn't even been allowed to help in planning the huts. Bbulas and some workmen had done all that themselves with the aid of some antique blueprints that had been put out centuries before by a Terrestrial magazine and had been acquired from a rare tape-and-book dealer on Gambrell, for, Skkiru thought, far too high a price. He could have designed them himself just as badly and much more cheaply.

It wasn't that Skkiru didn't understand well enough that Snaddra had been forced into making such a drastic change in its way of life. What resources it once possessed had been depleted and—aside from minerals—they had never been very extensive to begin with. All life-forms on the planet were on the point of extinction, save fish and rice—the only vegetable that would grow on Snaddra, and originally a Terran import at that. So food and fiber had to be brought from the other planets, at fabulous expense, for Snaddra was not on any of the direct trade routes and was too unattractive to lure the tourist business.

Something definitely had to be done, if it were not to decay altogether. And that was where the Planetary Dilettante came in.

*

The traditional office of Planetary Dilettante was a civil-service job, awarded by competitive examination whenever it fell vacant to the person who scored highest in intelligence, character and general gloonatz. However, the tests were inadequate when it came to measuring sense of proportion, adaptiveness and charm—and there, Skkiru felt, was where the essential flaw lay. After all, no really effective test would have let a person like Bbulas come out on top.

20

The winner was sent to Gambrell, the nearest planet with a Terran League University, to be given a thorough Terran-type education. No individual on Snaddra could afford such schooling, no matter how great his personal fortune, because the transportation costs were so immense that only a government could afford them. That was the reason why only one person in each generation could be chosen to go abroad at the planet's expense and acquire enough finish to cover the rest of the population.

The Dilettante's official function had always been, in theory, to serve the planet when an emergency came—and this, old Luccar, the former President, had decided, when he and the Parliament had awakened to the fact that Snaddra was falling into ruin, was an emergency. So he had, after considerable soul-searching, called upon Bbulas to plan a method of saving Snaddra—and Bbulas, happy to be in the limelight at last, had come up with this program.

It was not one Skkiru himself would have chosen. It was not one, he felt, that any reasonable person would have chosen. Nevertheless, the Bbulas Plan had been adopted by a majority vote of the Snaddrath, largely because no one had come up with a feasible alternative and, as a patriotic citizen, Skkiru would abide by it. He would accept the status of beggar; it was his duty to do so. Moreover, as in the case of the planet, there was no choice.

But all was not necessarily lost, he told himself. Had he not, in his anthropological viewings—though Bbulas might have been the only one privileged to go on ethnological field trips to other planets, he was not the only one who could use a library—seen accounts of societies where beggarhood could be a rewarding and even responsible station in life? There was no reason why, within the framework of the primitive society Bbulas had created to allure Terran anthropologists, Skkiru should not make something of himself and show that a beggar was worthy of the high priestess's hand—which would be entirely in the Terran primitive tradition of romance.

"Skkiru!" Bbulas was screaming, as he spun, now that the Terrans were out of ear- and eye-shot "Skkiru, you idiot, listen to me! What are those ridiculous things you are wearing on your silly feet?"

Skkiru protruded all of his eyes in innocent surprise. "Just some old pontoons I took from a wrecked air-car once. I have a habit of collecting junk and I thought—"

Bbulas twirled madly in the air. "You are not supposed to think. Leave all the thinking to me!"

"Yes, Bbulas," Skkiru said meekly.

*

He would have put up an argument, but he had bigger plans in mind and he didn't want them impeded in any way.

"But they seem like an excellent idea," Luccar suggested. "Primitive and yet convenient."

Bbulas slowed down and gulped. After all, in spite of the fact that he was now only chief yam-stealer—being prevented from practicing his profession simply because there were no yams on the planet and no one was quite certain what they were—Luccar had once been elected President by a large popular majority. And a large popular majority is decidedly a force to be reckoned with anywhere in the Galaxy.

"Any deviations arouse comment," Bbulas explained tightly.

"But if we all—"

"There would not be enough pontoons to go around, even if we stripped all the air-cars."

"I see," Luccar said thoughtfully. "We couldn't make—?"

"No time!" Bbulas snapped. "All right, Skkiru—get those things off your feet!"

"Will do," Skkiru agreed. It would be decidedly unwise to put up an argument now. So he'd get his feet muddy; it was all part of the higher good.

Later, as soon as the rain-dance rehearsals were under way, he slipped away. No part had been assigned to him anyhow, except that of onlooker, and he thought he could manage that without practice. He went down to the library, where, since all the attendants were aboveground, he could browse in the stacks to his hearts' content, without having to fill out numerous forms and be shoved about like a plagiarist or something.

If the Earthmen were interested in really primitive institutions, he thought, they should have a look at the city library. The filing system was really medieval. However, the library would, of course, be tabu for them, along with the rest of the city, which was not supposed to exist.

As far as the Terrans were to know, the group of lumpy stone huts (they should, properly speaking, have been wood, but wood was too rare and expensive) was the capital of Snaddra. It would be the capital of Snaddra for the Snaddrath, too, except during the hours of rest, when they would be permitted to retire unobtrusively to their cozy well-drained quarters beneath the mud. Life was going to be hard from now on—unless the Bbulas Plan moved faster than Bbulas himself had anticipated. And that would never happen without implementation from without. From without Bbulas, that was.

Skkiru got to work on the tex-tapes and soon decided upon his area of operations. Bbulas had concentrated so much effort on the ethos of the planet that he had devoted insufficient detail to the mythos.

THE IGNOBLE SAVAGES

That, therefore, was the field in which Skkiru felt he must concentrate. And concentrate he did.

*

The rain dance, which had been elaborately staged by the planet's finest choreographers, came to a smashing climax, after which there was a handsome display of fireworks.

"But it is still raining," Raoul protested.

"Did you expect the rain to stop?" Bbulas asked, his eyes bulging with involuntary surprise. "I mean—" he said, hastily retracting them—"well, it doesn't always stop right away. The gods may not have been feeling sufficiently propitious."

"Thought you had only one god, old boy," Cyril observed, after giving his associate a searching glance. "Chap by the name of Whipsnade or some such."

"Ipsnadd. He is our chief deity. But we have a whole pantheon. Major gods and minor gods. Heroes and demigods and nature spirits—"

"And do not forget the prophets," Larhgan put in helpfully. As former Chief Beauty of the planet (an elective civil-service office), she was not accustomed to being left out of things. "We have many prophets. And saints. I myself am studying to be a—"

Bbulas glared at her. Though her antennae quivered sulkily, she stopped and said no more—for the moment, anyway.

"Sounds like quite a complex civilization," Cyril commented.

"No, no!" Bbulas protested in alarm. "We are a simple primitive people without technological pretensions."

"You don't need any," Cyril assured him. "Not when you have fireworks that function in the rain."

Inside himself, Skkiru guffawed.

"We are a simple people," Bbulas repeated helplessly. "A very simple and very primitive people."

"Somehow," Raoul said, "I feel you may have a quality that civilization may have lost." The light in his eyes was recognizable to any even remotely humanoid species as a mystic glow.

But Cyril seemed well in command of the situation. "Come now, Raoul," he laughed, clapping his young colleague on the shoulder, "don't fall into the Rousseau trap—noble savage and all that sort of rot!"

"But that beggar!" Raoul insisted. "Trite, certainly, but incredible nonetheless! Before, one only read of such things—"

A glazed look came into two of Bbulas' eyes, while the third closed despairingly. "What beggar? What beggar? Tell me—I must know . . . as if I didn't really," he muttered in Snaddrath.

"The only beggar we've seen on this planet so far. That one."

*

With a wave of his hand, Cyril indicated the modest form of Skkiru, attempting to conceal himself behind Luccar's portly person.

"I realize it was only illusion, but, as my associate says, a remarkably good one. And," Cyril added, "an even more remarkable example of cultural diffusion."

"What do you mean? Please, gracious and lovable Terrans, deign to tell me what you mean. What did that insufferable beggar do?"

In spite of himself, Skkiru's knees flickered. *Fool*, he told himself, *you knew it was bound to come out sooner or later. Take courage in your own convictions; be convinced by your own courage. All he really can do is yell.*

"He did the Indian rope trick for us," Raoul explained. "And very well, too. Very well indeed."

25

THE IGNOBLE SAVAGES

"The—Indian rope trick!" Bbulas spluttered. "Why, the—" And then he recollected his religious vocation, as well as his supposed ignorance. "Would you be so kind as to tell me what the Indian rope trick is, good sirs?"

"Well, he did it with a chain, actually."

"We have no ropes on this planet," Larhgan contributed. "We are backward."

"And a small boy went up and disappeared," Raoul finished.

Suddenly forgetting the stiff-upper-lip training for which the planet had gone to such great expense, Bbulas spun around and around in a fit of bad temper, to Skkiru's great glee. Fortunately, the Dilettante retained enough self-control to keep his feet on the ground—perhaps remembering that to fail to do so would compound Skkiru's crime.

"Dervishism!" Raoul exclaimed, his eyes incandescent with interest. He pulled out his notebook. After biting his lip thoughtfully, Cyril did the same.

"Just like Skkiru!" Bbulas gasped as he spun slowly to a stop. "He is a disruptive cultural mechanism. Leading children astray!"

"But not at all," Raoul pointed out politely. "The boy came back unharmed and in the best of spirits."

"So far as we could see," Cyril amended. "Of course there may have been psychic damage."

"Which boy was it?" Bbulas demanded.

*

Cyril pointed to the urchin in question—a rather well-known juvenile delinquent, though the Terrestrials, of course, couldn't know that.

"He is a member of my own clan," Bbulas said. "He will be thrashed soundly."

"But why punish him?" Raoul asked. "What harm has he done?"

26

"Shhh," Cyril warned him. "You may be touching on a tabu. What's the matter with you, anyway? One would think you had forgotten every lesson you ever learned."

"Oh, I am truly sorry!" Raoul's face became a pleasing shade of pink, which made him look much more human. Maybe it was the wrong color, but at least it was a color. "Please to accept my apologies, reverend sir."

"It's quite all right." Bbulas reverted to graciousness. "The boy should not have associated with a beggar—especially that one. If he did not hold his post by time-hallowed tradition, we would—dispose of him. He has always been a trouble-maker."

"But I do not understand," Raoul persisted. Skkiru could not understand why Cyril did not stop him again. "The beggar did the trick very effectively. I know it was all illusion, but I should like to know just how he created such an illusion, and, moreover, how the Indian rope trick got all the way to—"

"It was all done by magic," Bbulas said firmly. "Magic outside the temple is not encouraged, because it is black magic, and so it is wrong. The magic of the priests is white magic, and so it is right. Put that down in your little book."

Raoul obediently wrote it down. "Still, I should like to know—"

"Let us speak of pleasanter things," Bbulas interrupted again. "Tomorrow night, we are holding a potlatch and we should be honored to have the pleasure of your company."

"Delighted," Raoul bowed.

"I was wrong," Cyril said. "This is not a remarkable example of cultural diffusion. It is a remarkable example of a diffuse culture."

*

"But I cannot understand," Raoul said to Cyril later, in the imagined privacy of their hut. "Why are you suspicious of this charming, friendly people, so like the natives that the textbooks lead one to expect?"

Naturally, Skkiru—having made his way in through a secret passage known only to the entire population of the city and explicitly designed for espionage, and was spying outside the door—thought, *we are textbook natives. Not only because we were patterned on literary prototypes, but because Bbulas never really left school—in spirit, anyway. He is the perpetual undergraduate and his whole scheme is nothing more than a grandiose Class Night.*

"Precisely what I've been thinking," Cyril said. "So like the textbooks—all the textbooks put together."

"What do you mean? Surely it is possible for analogous cultural features to develop independently in different cultures?"

"Oh, it's possible, all right. Probability—particularly when it comes to such a great number of features packed into one small culture—is another matter entirely."

"I cannot understand you," Raoul objected. "What do you want of these poor natives? To me, it seems everything has been of the most idyllic. Rapport was established almost immediately."

"A little too immediately, perhaps, don't you think? You haven't had much experience, Raoul, so you might not be aware it usually isn't as easy as this."

Cyril flung himself down on one of the cots that had been especially hardened for Terrestrial use and blew smoke rings at the ceiling. Skkiru was dying for a cigarette himself, but that was another cultural feature the Snaddrath had to dispense with now—not that smoking was insufficiently primitive, but that tobacco was not indigenous to the planet.

"That is because they are not a hostile people," Raoul insisted. "Apparently they have no enemies. Nonetheless, they are of the utmost interest. I hardly expected to land a society like this on my very first field trip," he added joyfully. "Never have I heard of so dynamic a culture! Never!"

"Nor I," Cyril agreed, "and this is far from being my very first field trip. It has a terribly large number of strange elements in it—strange, that is, when considered in relationship to the society as a whole. Environmental pressures seem to have had no effect upon their culture. For instance, don't you think it rather remarkable that a people with such an enormously complex social structure as theirs should wear clothing so ill adapted to protect them from the weather?"

*

"Well," Raoul pointed out enthusiastically—another undergraduate type, Skkiru observed, happiest with matters that either resembled those in books or came directly from them, so that they could be explicitly pigeonholed—"the Indians of Tierra del Fuego wore nothing but waist-length sealskin capes even in the bitterest cold. Of course, this civilization is somewhat more advanced than theirs in certain ways, but one finds such anomalies in all primitive civilizations, does one not?"

"That's true to a certain extent. But one would think they'd at least have developed boots to cope with the mud. And why was the beggar the only one to wear mudshoes? Why, moreover—" Cyril narrowed his eyes and pointed his cigarette at Raoul—"did he wear them only the first time and subsequently appear barefooted?"

"That *was* odd," Raoul admitted, "but—"

"And the high priest spoke of thrashing that boy. You should know, old chap, that cruelty to children is in inverse ratio to the degree of civilization."

THE IGNOBLE SAVAGES

Raoul stared at his colleague. "My faith, are you suggesting that we go see how hard they hit him, then?"

Cyril laughed. "All I suggest is that we keep a very open mind about this society until we can discover what fundamental attitudes are controlling such curious individual as well as group behavior."

"But assuredly. That is what we are here for, is it not? So why are you disturbing yourself so much?"

But it was Raoul, Skkiru thought, who appeared much more disturbed than Cyril. It was understandable—the younger man was interested only in straightforward ethnologizing and undoubtedly found the developing complications upsetting.

"Look," Cyril continued. "They call this place a hut. It's almost a palace."

My God, Skkiru thought, *what kind of primitive conditions are they used to?*

"That is largely a question of semantics," Raoul protested. "But regard—the roof leaks. Is that not backward enough for you, eh?" And Raoul moved to another part of the room to avoid receiving indisputable proof of the leakage on his person. "What is more, the sanitary arrangements are undeniably primitive."

"The roofs of many palaces leak, and there is no plumbing to speak of, and still they are not called huts. And tell me this—why should the metal-workers be the pariahs? Why *metal-workers?*"

Raoul's eyes opened wide. "You know there is often an outcast class with no apparent rationale behind its establishment. All the tapes—"

"True enough, but you will remember that the reason the smiths of Masai were pariahs was that they manufactured weapons which might tempt people to commit bloodshed. I keep remembering them, somehow. I keep remembering so many things here. . . . "

"But we have seen no weapons on this planet," Raoul argued. "In fact, the people seem completely peaceful."

"Right you are." Cyril blew another smoke ring. "Since this is a planet dependent chiefly upon minerals, why make the members of its most important industry the out-group?"

"You think it is that they may be secretly hostile?"

Cyril smiled. "I think they may be secretly something, but hardly hostile."

Aha, Skkiru thought. *Bbulas, my splendidly scaled friend, I will have something interesting to tell you.*

*

"You idiot!" Bbulas snarled later that night, as most of the Snaddrath met informally in the council chamber belowground, the new caste distinctions being, if not forgotten, at least in abeyance—for everyone except Bbulas. "You imbecile!" He whirled, unable to repress his Snadd emotions after a long behaviorally Terran day. "I have half a mind to get rid of you by calling down divine judgment."

"How would you do that?" Skkiru demanded, emboldened by the little cry of dismay, accompanied by a semi-somersault, which Larhgan gave. In spite of everything, she still loved him; she would never belong to Bbulas, though he might plan until he was ochre in the face.

"Same way you did the rope trick. Only you wouldn't come back, my boy. Nice little cultural trait for the ethnologists to put in their peace pipes and smoke. Never saw such people for asking awkward questions." Bbulas sighed and straightened his antennae with his fingers, since their ornaments made them too heavy to allow reflective verticalization. "Reminds me of final exams back on Gambrell."

THE IGNOBLE SAVAGES

"Anthropologists *always* ask awkward questions—everybody knows that," Larhgan put in. "It's their function. And I don't think you should speak that way to Skkiru, Bbulas. Like all of us, he's only trying to do his best. No man—or woman—can do more."

She smiled at Skkiru and his hearts whirled madly inside him. Only a dolt, he thought, would give way to despair; there was no need for this intolerable situation to endure for a lifetime. If only he could solve the problem more quickly than Bbulas expected or—Skkiru began to understand—wanted, Larhgan could be his again.

"With everybody trying to run this planet," Bbulas snarled, taking off his headdress, "no wonder things are going wrong."

Luccar intervened. Although it was obvious that he had been enjoying to a certain extent the happy anonymity of functionless yam-stealer, old elective responsibilities could not but hang heavy over a public servant of such unimpeachable integrity.

"After all," the old man said, "secretly we're still a democracy, and secretly I am still President, and secretly I'm beginning to wonder if perhaps we weren't a little rash in—"

"Look here, all of you," Bbulas interrupted querulously. "I'm not doing this for my own amusement."

*

But that's just what you are doing, Skkiru thought, *even though you wouldn't admit it to yourself, nor would you think of it as amusement.*

"You know what happened to Nemeth," Bbulas continued, using an argument that had convinced them before, but that was beginning to wear a little thin now. "Poorest, most backward planet in the whole Galaxy. A couple of ethnologists from Earth stumbled on it a little over a century ago and what happened? More kept on coming; the trade ships followed. Now it's the richest, most advanced planet in that whole sector. There's no reason why the same thing can't happen to us in this sector, if we play our cards carefully."

"But maybe these two won't tell other anthropologists about us," Luccar said. "Something the older one remarked certainly seemed to imply as much. Maybe they don't want the same thing to happen again—in which case, all this is a waste of time. Furthermore," he concluded rather petulantly, "at my age, I don't like running about in the open; it's not healthful."

"If they don't tell other anthropologists about us," Bbulas said, his face paling to lime-green with anxiety, "we can spread the news unobtrusively ourselves. Just let one study be published, even under false coordinates, and we can always hire a good public relations man to let our whereabouts leak out. Please, everybody, stick to your appointed tasks and let me do the worrying. You haven't even given this culture a chance! It's hardly more than a day old and all I hear are complaints, complaints, complaints."

"You'd better worry," Skkiru said smugly, "because already those Terrans think there's something fishy about this culture. Ha, ha! Did you get that—fishy?"

Only Larhgan laughed. She loved him.

"How do you know they're suspicious?" Bbulas demanded. "Are you in their confidence? Skkiru, if you've been talking—"

"All I did was spy outside their door," Skkiru said hastily. "I knew *you* couldn't eavesdrop; it wouldn't look dignified if you were caught. But beggars do that kind of thing all the time. And I wanted to show you I could be of real use."

He beamed at Larhgan, who beamed back.

"I could have kept my findings to myself," he went on, "but I came to tell you. In fact—" he dug in his robe—"I even jotted down a few notes."

33

THE IGNOBLE SAVAGES

"It wasn't at all necessary, Skkiru," Bbulas said in a tired voice. "We took the elementary precaution of wiring their hut for sound and a recorder is constantly taking down their every word."

"Hut!" Skkiru kept his antennae under control with an effort, but his retort was feeble. "They think it's a palace. You did them too well, Bbulas."

"I may have overdone the exterior architecture a bit," the high priest admitted. "Not that it seems relevant to the discussion. Although I've been trying to arrange our primitivism according to Terrestrial ideas of cultural backwardness, I'm afraid many of the physical arrangements are primitive according to our conceptions rather than theirs."

*

"Why *must* we be primitive according to Terran ideas?" Luccar wanted to know. "Why must we be slaves even to fashions in backwardness?"

"Hear, hear!" cried an anonymous voice.

"And thank you, Skkiru," the former President continued, "for telling me they were suspicious. I doubt that Bbulas would have taken the trouble to inform me of so trivial a matter."

"As high priest," Bbulas said stiffly, "I believe the matter, trivial or not, now falls within my province."

"Shame!" cried an anonymous voice—or it might have been the same one.

Bbulas turned forest-green and his antennae twitched. "After all, you yourself, Luccar, agreed to accept the role of elder statesman—"

"Yam-stealer," Luccar corrected him bitterly, "which is not the same thing."

"On Earth, it is. And," Bbulas went on quickly, "as for our assuming primitive Earth attitudes, where else are we going to get our

34

attitudes from? We can't borrow any primitive attitudes from Nemeth, because they're too well known. And since there are no other planets we know of with intelligent life-forms that have social structures markedly different from the major Terran ones—except for some completely non-humanoid cultures, which, for physiological reasons, we are incapable of imitating—we have to rely upon records of primitive Terran sources for information. Besides, a certain familiarity with the traits manifested will make the culture more understandable to the Terrans, and, hence, more attractive to them psychologically." He stopped and straightened out his antennae.

"In other words," Skkiru commented, emboldened by a certain aura of sympathy he felt emanating from Larhgan, at least, and probably from Luccar, too, "he doesn't have the imagination to think up any cultural traits for himself, so he has to steal them—and that's the easiest place to steal them from."

"This is none of your business, Skkiru," Bbulas snapped. "You just beg."

"It's the business of all of us, Bbulas," Luccar corrected softly. "Please to remember that, no matter what our alloted roles, we are all concerned equally in this."

"Of course, of course, but please let me handle the situation in my own way, since I made the plans. And, Skkiru," the Dilettante added with strained grace, "you may have a warm cloak to wear as soon as we can get patches welded on."

Then Bbulas took a deep breath and reverted to his old cheer-leader manner. "Now we must all get organized for the potlatch. We can give the Terrans those things the Ladies' Aid has been working on all year for the charity bazaar and, in exchange, perhaps they will give us more chocolate bars—" he glanced reproachfully at Skkiru—"and other food."

THE IGNOBLE SAVAGES

"And perhaps some yams," Luccar suggested, "so that—God save us—I can steal them."

"I'll definitely work on that," Bbulas promised.

*

Skkiru was glad that, as beggar, he held no prominent position at the feast—in reality, no position at all—for he hated fish. And fish, naturally, would be the chief refreshment offered, since the Snaddrath did not want the Terrans to know that they had already achieved that degrading dependency upon the tin can that marks one of the primary differences between savagery and civilization.

There were fish pâté on rice crackers, fish soup with rice, boiled fish, baked fish, fried fish and a pilau of rice with fish. There were fish chitlins, fish chips, fish cakes, fish candy and guslat—a potent distillation of fermented fish livers—to wash it all down. And even in the library, where Skkiru sought refuge from the festivities, fishy fumes kept filtering down through the ventilating system to assail his nostrils.

Bbulas had been right in a way, Skkiru had to admit to himself upon reflection. In trying to improve his lot, Skkiru had taken advantage of the Snaddrath's special kinetic talents, which had been banned for the duration—and so he had, in effect, committed a crime.

This time, however, he would seek to uplift himself in terms acceptable to the Terrans on a wholly indigenous level, and in terms which would also hasten the desired corruptive process—in a nice way, of course—so that the Snaddrath civilization could be profitably undermined as fast as possible and Larhgan be his once again. It was a hard problem to solve, but he felt sure he could do it. Anything Bbulas could do, he could do better.

Then he had it! And the idea was so wonderful that he was a little sorry at the limited range it would necessarily cover. His part really should be played out before a large, yoomping audience, but he was realistic enough to see that it would be most expedient for him to give a private performance for the Earthmen alone.

On the other hand, he now knew it should be offered outside the hut, because the recorder would pick up his cries and Bbulas would be in a spin—as he would be about any evidence of independent thinking on the planet. Bbulas was less interested in the planet's prospering, it was now clear to Skkiru, than in its continuing in a state where he would remain top fish.

*

Fortunately, the guslat had done its work, and by the time the Earthmen arrived at the door to their hut, they were alone. The rest of the company either had fallen into a stupor or could not trust themselves to navigate the mud.

The Earthmen—with an ingeniousness which would have augured well for the future development of their race, had it not already been the (allegedly) most advanced species in the Galaxy—had adapted some spare parts from their ship into replicas of Skkiru's mudshoes. They did, in truth, seem none too steady on their feet, but he was unable to determine to what degree this was a question of intoxication and what degree a question of navigation.

"Alms, for the love of Ipsnadd." He thrust forward his begging bowl.

"Regard, it is the beggar! Why were you not at the festivities, worthy mendicant?" Raoul hiccuped. "Lovely party. Beautiful women. Delicious fish."

THE IGNOBLE SAVAGES

Skkiru started to stand on his head, then remembered this was no longer a socially acceptable expression of grief and cast his eyes down. "I was not invited," he said sadly.

"Like the little match girl," Raoul sympathized. "My heart bleeds for you, good match gi—good beggar. Does your heart not bleed for him, Cyril?"

"Bad show," the older ethnologist agreed, with a faint smile. "But that's what you've got to expect, if you're going to be a primitive."

He was very drunk, Skkiru decided; he must be, to phrase his sentiments so poorly. Unless he—but no, Skkiru refused to believe that. He didn't mind Cyril's being vaguely suspicious, but that was as far as he wanted him to go. Skkiru's toes apprehensively started to quiver.

"How can you say a thing like that to a primitive?" Raoul demanded. "If he were not a primitive, it would be all right to call him a primitive, but one does not accuse primitives of being primitives. It's—it's downright primitive; that's what it is!"

"You need some coffee, my boy." Cyril grinned. "Black coffee. That guslat of theirs is highly potent stuff."

They were about to go inside. Skkiru had to act quickly. He slumped over. Although he had meant to land on the doorstep, he lacked the agility to balance himself with the precision required and so he fell smack into the mud. The feel of the slime on his bare feet had been bad enough; oozing over his skin through the interstices of his clothing, it was pure hell. What sacrifices he was making for his planet! And for Larhgan. The thought of her would have to sustain him through this viscous ordeal, for there was nothing else solid within his grasp.

"Ubbl," he said, lifting his head from the ooze, so that they could see the froth coming out of his mouth. "Glubbl."

*

Raoul clutched Cyril. "What is he doing?"

"Having an epileptic fit, I rather fancy. Go on, old man," Cyril said to Skkiru. "You're doing splendidly. Splendidly!"

"I see the sky!" Skkiru howled, anxious to get his prophecies over with before he sank any deeper in the mud. "It is great magic. I see many ships in the sky. They are all coming to Snaddra. . . . "

"Bearing anthropologists and chocolate bars, I suppose," murmured Cyril.

"Shhh," Raoul said indignantly. "You must not interrupt. He is having personal contact with the supernatural, a very important element of the primitive ethos."

"Thank you," Cyril said. "I'll try to remember that."

So will I, thought Skkiru. "They carry learned men and food for the spiritually and physically hungry people of Snaddra," he interrupted impatiently. "They carry warm clothing for the poor and miserable people of Snaddra. They carry yams for the larcenous and frustrated people of Snaddra."

"Yams!" Raoul echoed. "*Yams!*"

"Shhh, this is fascinating. Go on, beggar."

But the mud sogging over Skkiru's body was too much. The fit could be continued at a later date—and in a drier location.

"Where am I?" he asked, struggling to a sitting position.

"You are on Snaddra, fifth planet of the sun Weebl," Raoul began, "in—"

"Weeeeebl," Skkiru corrected, getting to his feet with the older ethnologist's assistance. "What happened?" He beat futilely at the mud caught in the meshes of his metal rags. "I feel faint."

"Come in and have some coffee with us," Cyril invited. This also was part of Skkiru's plan, for he had no intention of going back across that mud, if he could possibly help it. He had nothing further to say that the recorders should not hear. Bbulas might object to his associating with the Earthmen, but he couldn't do much if the association seemed entirely innocent. At the moment, Snaddra might be a theocracy, but the democratic hangover was still strong.

"I would rather have some hot chocolate," Skkiru said. "That is, if you have no objection to drinking with a beggar."

"My dear fellow—" Cyril put an arm around Skkiru's muddy shoulders—"we ethnologists do not hold with caste distinctions. Come in and have chocolate—with a spot of rum, eh? That'll make you right as a trivet in a matter of seconds."

*

It wasn't until much later, after several cups of the finest chocolate he had ever tasted, that Skkiru announced himself to feel quite recovered.

"Please do not bother to accompany me to the door," he said. "I can find my own way. You do me too much honor. I would feel shamefaced."

"But—" Cyril began.

"No," Skkiru said. "It is—it is bad form here. I insist. I must go my way alone."

"All right," Cyril agreed.

Raoul looked at him in some surprise.

"All right," Cyril repeated in a louder tone. "Go by yourself, if an escort would bother you. But please give the door a good bang, so the lock will catch."

Skkiru slammed the door lustily to simulate the effect of departure and then he descended via the secret passage inside the hut itself, scrabbling a little because the hot chocolate seemed strangely to have affected his sense of balance.

The rest of the Snaddrath were in the council chamber gloating over the loot from the potlatch. It was, as a matter of fact, a good take.

"Where were you, Skkiru?" Bbulas asked, examining a jar of preserved kumquats suspiciously. "Up to no good, I'll be bound."

"Oh, my poor Skkiru!" Larhgan exclaimed, before Skkiru could say anything. "How muddy and wretched-looking you are! I don't like this whole thing," she told Bbulas. "It's cruel. Being high priestess isn't nearly as much fun as I thought it would be."

"This is not supposed to be fun," the Dilettante informed her coldly. "It is in dead earnest. Since the question has been brought up, however, what did happen to you, Skkiru?"

"I—er—fell down and, being a beggar, I had no other garments to change into."

"You'll survive," Bbulas said unfeelingly. "On Earth, I understand, people fall into mud all the time. Supposed to have a beneficial effect—and any effect on you, Skkiru, would have to be beneficial."

Larhgan was opening her mouth to say something—probably, Skkiru thought fondly, in his defense—when there came a thud and a yell from the passage outside. Two yells, in fact. And two thuds.

"My faith," exclaimed a Terrestrial voice, "but how did the beggar descend! I am sure every bone in my body is broken."

"I think you'll find him possessed of means of locomotion not known to us. But you're not hurt, old chap—only bruised."

And Cyril came into the council chamber, followed by a limping Raoul. "Good evening, ladies and gentlemen. I trust this is not an intrusion, although I'm quite sure you'll tell us we've broken a whole slue of tabus."

"You!" Bbulas screamed at Skkiru. "You must have used the passage in the hut! You let them follow you!"

THE IGNOBLE SAVAGES

Losing control of his own reflexes, he began to whirl madly.

*

"But regard this!" Raoul exclaimed, staring around him. "To build a place like this beneath the mud—name of a name, these people must have hydraulic engineering far superior to anything on Earth!"

"You are too kind," the former hydraulic engineer said deprecatingly. "Actually, it's quite simple—"

"This is not a primitive civilization at all, Raoul," Cyril explained. "They've been faking it from tapes. Probably have a culture very much like ours, with allowances for climatic differences, of course. Oh, undoubtedly it would be provincial, but—"

"We are not provincial," Larhgan said coldly. "Primitive, yes. Provincial, no! We are—"

"But why should they do a thing like this to us?" Raoul wailed.

"I imagine they did it to get on the trade routes, as Nemeth did. They've been trying not to talk about Nemeth all the while. Must have been rather a strain. You ought to be ashamed of yourselves!" Cyril told the assembled Snaddrath. "Very bad form!"

Bbulas was turning paler and paler as he whirled. "All your fault," he gasped hoarsely to Skkiru. "All your fault!"

And that was true, Skkiru realized. His antennae quivered, but he didn't even try to restrain them. He had meant well, yet he had messed up the planet's affairs far more seriously than Bbulas had. He had ruined their hopes, killed all their chances by his carelessness. He, Skkiru, instead of being his planet's savior, was its spoiler. He psonked violently.

But Larhgan moved nearer to him. "It's all over, anyhow," she whispered, "and you know what? I'm glad. I'm glad we failed. I'd rather starve as myself than succeed as a sham."

42

Skkiru controlled himself. Silently, he took the grimpatch out of his carrier and, as silently, she took it back.

"My faith, they must have had plumbing all the time!" Raoul complained.

"Very likely," said Cyril sternly. "Looks as if we've suffered for nothing."

"Such people!" Raoul said. "True primitives, I am sure, would never have behaved so unfeelingly!"

Cyril smiled, but his face was hard as he turned back to the Snaddrath. "We'll radio Gambrell in the morning to have a ship dispatched to pick us up. I'm not sure but that we have a good case for fraud against you."

"We're destroyed!" Bbulas shrieked as the full emotional impact of the situation hit him. "An interplanetary lawsuit would ruin Snaddra entirely."

His cries were echoed in the howls of the other Snaddrath, their antennae psonking, their eyes bulging.

*

Agonized by his sorrow, Bbulas lost all emotional restraint, forgot about his Terrestrial training, and turned upside down in a spasm of grief. Since there was no longer any reason to repress their natural manifestation of feeling, all the Snaddrath followed suit, their antennae twisting in frenzy as they ululated.

And then, to Skkiru's surprise and the surprise of all the rest, Cyril stopped and took out his notebook. "Wait a minute," he said as Raoul did likewise. All four Earthly eyes were shining with a glow that was recognizable to any even remotely humanoid species as the glow of intellectual fervor. "Wait just a minute! Our plans are altered. We may stay, after all!"

THE IGNOBLE SAVAGES

One by one, the Snaddrath reversed to upright positions, but did not retract their eyes, for they were still staring at the Earthmen. Skkiru knew now what had been bothering him about the Terrestrials all along. They were crazy—that was what it was. Who but maniacs would want to leave their warm, dry planets and go searching the stars for strange cultures, when they could stay quietly at home in peace and comfort with their families?

Skkiru's hand reached out for Larhgan's and found it.